The stories in this collection were previously published individually by Candlewick Press.
These books are based on the TV series *Peppa Pig*.
Peppa Pig is created by Neville Astley and Mark Baker.
Peppa Pig © Astley Baker Davies/Entertainment One U.K. Ltd 2003.
www.peppapig.com

First compilation edition in this format 2020
Library of Congress Cataloging-in-Publication Data is available for the individual hardcover editions.

Peppa Pig and the Muddy Puddles
Library of Congress Catalog Card Number 2012942611
ISBN 978-0-7636-6523-4 (2013 hardcover)

Peppa Pig and the Great Vacation
Library of Congress Catalog Card Number 2013944083
ISBN 978-0-7636-6986-7 (2014 hardcover)

Peppa Pig and the Busy Day at School
Library of Congress Catalog Card Number 2012947254
ISBN 978-0-7636-6525-8 (2013 hardcover)

Peppa Pig and the Library Visit
Library of Congress Catalog Card Number 2017956983
ISBN 978-0-7636-9788-4 (2017 hardcover)

Peppa Pig and the Day at the Museum
Library of Congress Catalog Card Number 2014952809
ISBN 978-0-7636-8060-2 (2015 hardcover)

Peppa Pig and the Treasure Hunt
Library of Congress Catalog Card Number 2014939354
ISBN 978-0-7636-7703-9 (2015 hardcover)

ISBN 978-1-5362-1338-6 (hardcover collection)

20 21 22 23 24 APS 10 9 8 7 6 5 4 3 2

Printed in Humen, Dongguan, China

This book was typeset in Peppa.
The illustrations were created digitally.

Candlewick Entertainment
an imprint of Candlewick Press
99 Dover Street
Somerville, Massachusetts 02144

visit us at www.candlewick.com

STORY
TREASURY

CANDLEWICK
ENTERTAINMENT

Contents

Peppa Pig
and the
Muddy Puddles

Mummy Pig and Daddy Pig are tucking Peppa and George into bed.

"There's so much rain!" Peppa says.
"That means there will be muddy puddles to jump in tomorrow,"
Mummy Pig says with a smile.

The *splish-splash-splosh* of raindrops on the window sings Peppa and George to sleep. They dream of muddy puddles.

3

It rains . . .

and rains . . .

and rains.

The next morning, the sun is shining.
Daddy Pig runs out to jump in a muddy puddle.
But he lands in a big pool of water instead!

"Oh! How did this water get here?" Daddy Pig asks.

"And where are the muddy puddles?" asks Peppa.

Splash!

Quack!
Quack!
Quack!

"Our house is on an island!"
says Peppa.

"Oh, dear," says Mummy Pig.
"What will we do?"

Granny Pig and Grandpa Pig arrive on their boat.
"Ahoy, there!" Grandpa Pig says. "Wonderful boating weather!"

"We're going to the store," says Granny Pig.

"Can George and I come, too?" asks Peppa.

"Yes! We'll do the shopping for everybody!"

Squawk!

"Polly can remember our shopping list.
She's very good at that,"
Granny Pig says.
"Who's a clever parrot?"

"SQUAWK!
Who's a clever parrot?"
says Polly.
Polly is very good at
repeating what people say.

Peppa, George, Grandpa Pig, Granny Pig, and Polly motor across the water. It's fun, but there are no muddy puddles.

Each house is on its own island.
They go from house to house, asking everyone what
they need from the store.

Suzy Sheep
asks for chocolate.

"SQUAWK! Chocolate!" Polly repeats.

Granddad Dog needs a newspaper,
and Danny Dog wants a comic book.

"SQUAWK! Newspaper!
Comic book!" Polly repeats.

Grampy Rabbit wants cheese.

"SQUAWK! Cheese!"
Polly repeats.

Grandpa Pig's boat arrives at the supermarket.

"Hello!" says Miss Rabbit. "What can I get you?"

"Polly knows!" Peppa says proudly.

Squawk!

Polly opens her beak.
"Who's a clever parrot?
Who's a clever parrot?" she says.
Polly has forgotten the list!

"Don't worry," says Peppa. "I remember. . . ."

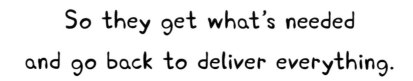

So they get what's needed
and go back to deliver everything.

"**Cheese**," says Grampy Rabbit.
"Thank you!"

"**A newspaper**
and **comic book**," say
Granddad Dog and Danny Dog.
"Thank you!"

"Chocolate!" says Suzy Sheep. "Thank you!"

"Chocolate for dinner?" asks Mummy Sheep.

Peppa and George are very sleepy when they arrive back home.

"Did you have fun?" asks Mummy Pig.

"Yes," says Peppa. "We got lots of things at the store.
We got something for everyone."

Snort!

But Peppa is sad.

She didn't get what *she* wanted.

There were no muddy puddles at all.

The next morning,
the sun is shining brightly
in the clear blue sky.
Polly Parrot comes to visit.

Grandpa Pig's boat is stuck
on Peppa's front lawn!

"Oh!" Granny Pig says,
looking out from the boat.
"The flood is over!"

They all look around.

The houses that were on islands yesterday
are now back to normal,
sitting on top of their hills.

The water that Peppa
and George boated in
is gone.

And at the bottom
of their very own hill they see . . .

24

Hee! Hee!

Squelch!

a great big

muddy puddle . . .

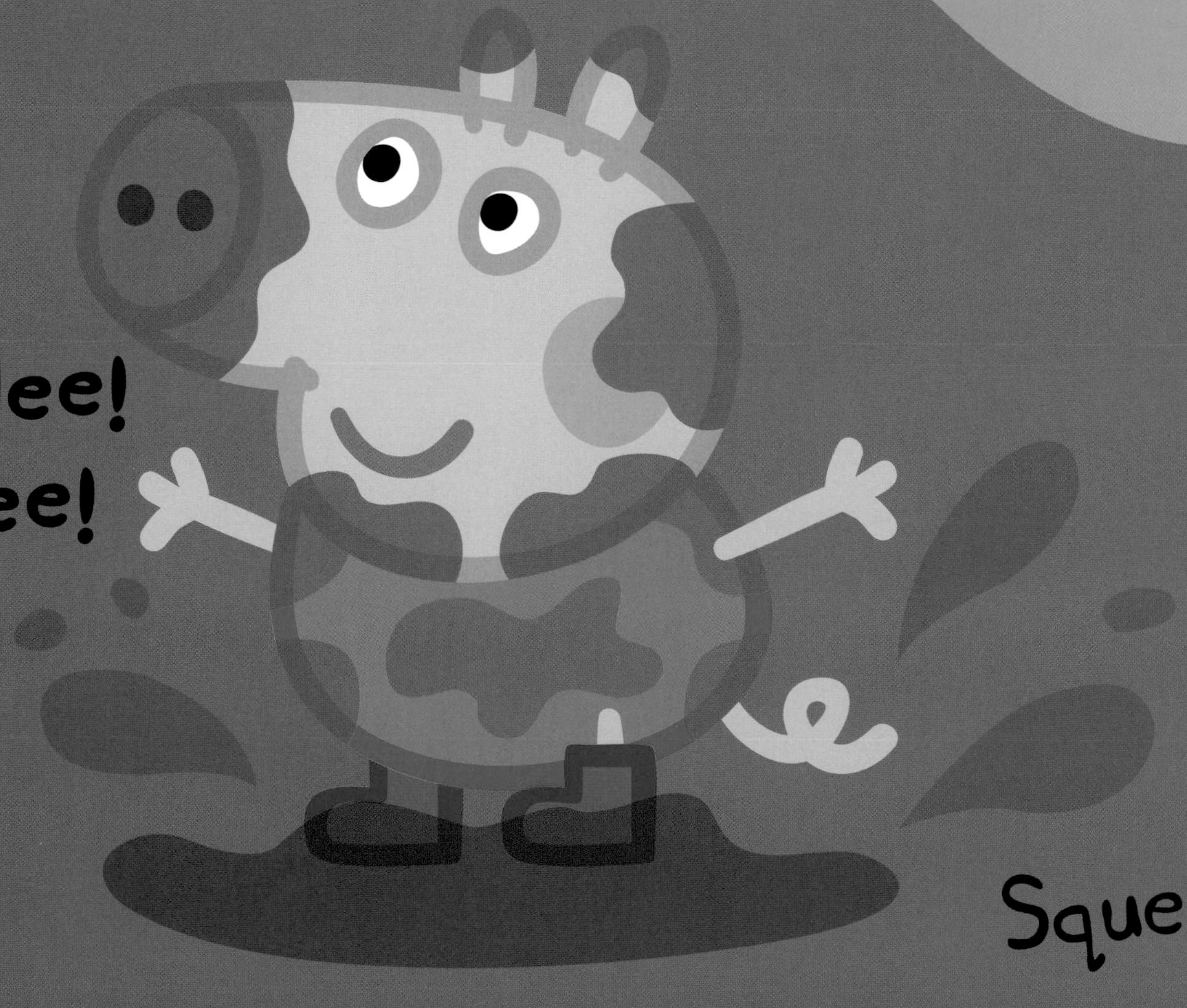

big enough
for everyone!

Peppa Pig

and the
Great Vacation

Peppa Pig and George are packing to go on vacation.

"You can't bring everything," says Daddy Pig.

"But we need all our toys!" says Peppa.

"Just your favorites," says Daddy Pig.

Peppa brings Teddy.

George brings his dinosaur.
"Dine-saw! *Grrrr*," says George.

"Can Goldie come, too?" asks Peppa.

"Sorry, Peppa, Goldie can't join us. But Granny Pig
and Grandpa Pig will look after her."

The car is packed, and the family is on the road.
"When will we get there?" calls Peppa from the backseat.
Daddy Pig tells Peppa that they have a long drive.

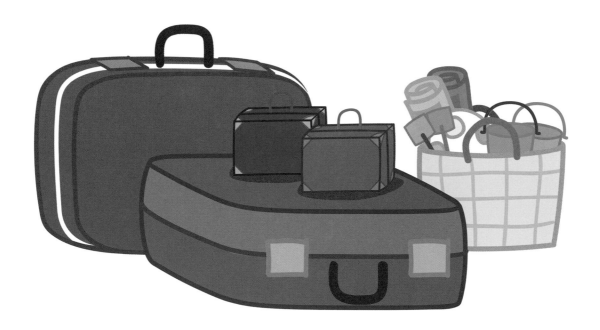

They head out to the
countryside and on
to a rented vacation
house near the ocean.

At the vacation house, Mummy Pig unpacks her suitcase.
She brought a lot of things!

"I miss Goldie," says Peppa. "Do you think she's all right?"

"I think so," says Mummy Pig.

Peppa calls Grandpa Pig just to make sure.

The next morning is very sunny and warm.
"Perfect day for a walk," says Daddy Pig.

"Daddy, you found the pool!" calls Peppa.

"Yes," says Daddy Pig. "I did."

Mummy Pig goes shopping in town.

Peppa and George want to have pizza for lunch.

Mummy Pig has found some presents for Granny Pig and Grandpa Pig.

"That won't all fit in your suitcase," says Daddy Pig.

"I want to get something, too," says Peppa.

"I hope it's small," says Daddy Pig.

"It is," says Peppa. "It's a postcard. And it doesn't have to go in a suitcase. It will go in the mail."

The next day,

Peppa and her family go on a nature walk.

Daddy Pig has packed a big picnic lunch.
"There's nothing here but trees," says Peppa.

"Look around, Peppa," says Mummy Pig.
"There is lots to see here."

Peppa looks around. "Tracks!" she says.
"I see tracks!"

"Dine-saw?" asks George.

"No, George,
not dinosaur tracks,"
says Peppa.

The tracks come to an end.
Peppa gets Daddy Pig's binoculars and looks up.
"I see birds. A mother and babies in a nest."

Peppa likes looking through the binoculars.
Next she looks down.
"I see ants," she says.
"They're carrying leaves
for lunch. Ant salad!"

"Yuck," says George.

Peppa is hungry.
So are Mummy Pig
and Daddy Pig and
George. Time for
a nice picnic lunch.
Peppa can't wait
to tell Granny Pig
and Grandpa Pig what
a nice day they had
on the nature walk.

That evening, Peppa calls Grandpa Pig.
He promises to tell Goldie that Peppa misses her
and that she will be home soon.

"We're taking good care of her," he says.

The next day,

Daddy Pig and Mummy Pig take Peppa and George to the beach.

It's a sandy beach with lots of rocks.
Peppa finds a shell. George finds a fossil!
Daddy Pig finds a crab. "There's a tide pool!" says Peppa.

Peppa and George look in the tiny pool. There are small plants.
"There's a gold coin!" says Peppa.
"Oooh," says George.

Something is making bubbles.
What could it be?

"A fish!" says Peppa.

"Hello, fish. You would love my fish, Goldie!"

Vacation is nearly over.

Time to pack the suitcases and get back in the car.

It's a long drive home, but Peppa has Teddy
to keep her company in the backseat. She has George, too.
It has been a great vacation—but she can't wait to see Goldie!

Mummy Pig gives Granny Pig her present.

Peppa runs to see Goldie.
"Oh, you've grown," she says. "A lot."

"She seemed hungry," says Grandpa Pig.

Mr. Zebra arrives. "I have a postcard all
the way from the beach," he says.

"Look, Goldie," says Peppa.
"You've got mail—something from our great vacation!"

Peppa Pig

and the

Busy Day at School

It's Special Talent Day at school,

and Peppa is very excited. She has many different talents,
so she hasn't decided which one to share.

"Maybe I will jump rope,"
says Peppa.

"Or sing or dance."

Mummy Pig, Daddy Pig, Peppa, and
George eat a good pancake breakfast.
Then they get in the car
and go to school.

Peppa's friends have already arrived. Pedro Pony, Candy Cat, and Rebecca Rabbit are there.

"Good morning," says Madame Gazelle. "Are you ready for Special Talent Day? We'll share our talents this afternoon. But first we have a busy day."

The class
practices counting.

"One, two, three,
four, five,"
begins Madame
Gazelle.

"SIX,
SEVEN,
EIGHT,
NINE,
TEN!"
shouts the class.

Then Madame Gazelle asks the class to name things that begin with each letter of the alphabet.

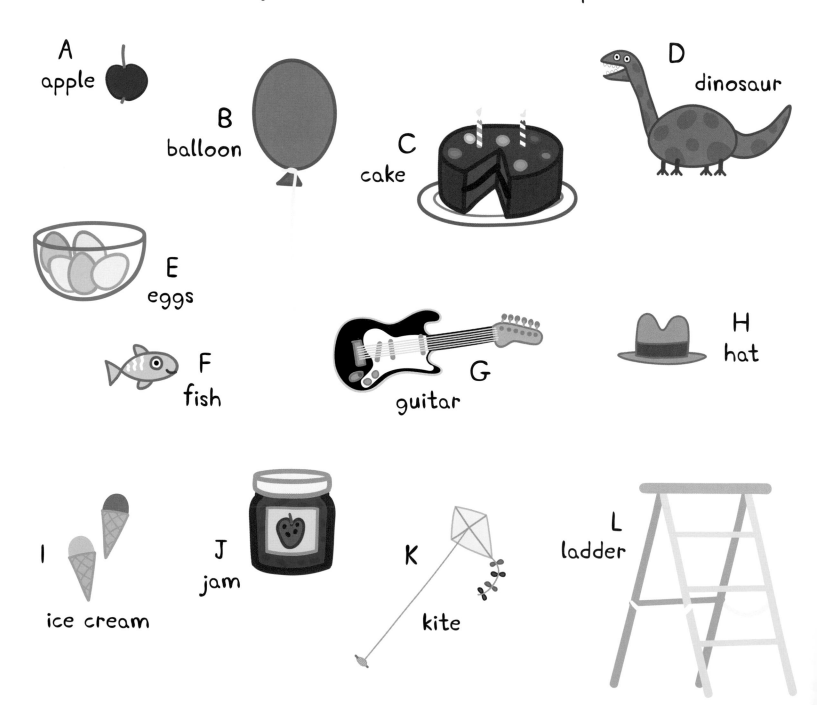

A apple

B balloon

C cake

D dinosaur

E eggs

F fish

G guitar

H hat

I ice cream

J jam

K kite

L ladder

M
monkey

N
newspaper

O
owl

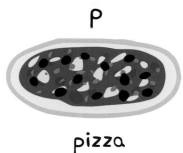
P
pizza

Q
queen

R
rocket

S
scooter

T
truck

U
umbrella

V
violin

W
watermelon

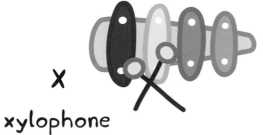
X
xylophone

Y
yarn

Z
Zoe Zebra!

Then it's time to play store.
Peppa and Suzy are the shopkeepers.

"What would you like?" asks Peppa.
"Do you have any cookies?" asks Danny Dog.
"No," says Peppa, "but we do have a toy telephone.
That will be one dollar."
"Thank you," says Danny Dog.

"Do you have a loaf of bread?"
asks Pedro Pony.
"No," says Peppa,
"but we do have a dollhouse!"
"Well, okay," says Pedro.

"What can I buy for a hundred dollars?"
asks Rebecca Rabbit.
"How about a carrot?" says Peppa.
Everyone laughs.

Next it's time to paint.

Peppa wants to teach George how to paint a flower.

"Make a circle," says Peppa.

George paints a green circle.
Then he paints a green zigzag line.

"That's not right, George," says Peppa.
George keeps painting.

Madame Gazelle looks
at Peppa's painting.
"What a lovely flower,"
she says.

"And George has
painted a dinosaur.
Perfect!"

At lunchtime, Peppa and George eat sandwiches with Danny Dog. There's watermelon for dessert!

Hooray!

Recess!

Everyone heads outside to the playground.

There's a new tire swing and Peppa wants to try it. She squeezes in.

"Help!" she cries. "I'm stuck!"

Peppa looks funny in the swing.

But Peppa doesn't think being stuck is funny. Her friends try to help.

They pull and pull and pull. Pop! Out comes Peppa!

"Let's play on the slide," she says.

"It's time for **music, music, music!**" sings Madame Gazelle. "Everyone choose an instrument."

Danny chooses the bongo drums.

"Look, I've got cymbals," says Rebecca.

Zoe gets maracas, Freddy chooses a triangle, and Pedro has a tambourine.

Everyone plays together: **Boom, bang, crash!**

"Oh, my!" cries Madame Gazelle.

"That sounds a bit more like noise than music!"

Bang, bang, bang

go the bongo drums.

Crash, crash, crash, go the cymbals.

Shake-a, shake-a, shake-a go the maracas.

"Lovely!" says Madame Gazelle.

Finally, it is time for Special Talents.
Everyone takes a turn.

Danny Dog's special talent is drumming.

Bang, bang, bang.

Pedro Pony does a magic trick.
Everyone closes their eyes, and
he makes a glass of water disappear.

Zoe Zebra sings.

Candy Cat jumps rope.

Oh, no, thinks Peppa. Now I can't do either of those.

It's a good thing I'm good at dancing, too!

Then Suzy Sheep gets up. "I'm going to dance," she says.

"Oh, no," says Peppa.

"What's the matter?" asks Madame Gazelle.

"I don't have a special talent
that hasn't been done already,"
says Peppa.

"Of course you do," says Madame Gazelle.
"Think of something you really like to do."

Peppa is quiet. She thinks. Then she smiles.
"I know!" she says. She grabs her boots. "Follow me!"

"I'm the best at jumping in muddy puddles!"

Peppa jumps
in a muddy puddle.

Then everyone jumps
in muddy puddles!

"This has been a very good day at school," says Peppa.

And it has.

Peppa Pig

and the
Library Visit

It's bedtime for Peppa and George.

"Could we have a story, please?"

asks Peppa.

"Okay," says Mummy Pig.
"Here's the one about the red monkey."

"We always read that one," says Peppa.
"The red monkey takes a bath,

brushes his teeth,

and goes to sleep.
Let's choose another book instead."

Peppa goes to the bookshelf.

There's a book about a **blue tiger**,

a book about a
green spider,

a book about an
orange
penguin,
and . . .

"Ooh!" says Peppa.
"What's **this** one?"

"*The Wonderful World
of Concrete,*"
reads Mummy Pig.

"I've been looking for
that!" says Daddy Pig.
"It's a book I borrowed
from the library."

"**What's a library?**" asks Peppa.

"A library is a place you can go to borrow books.
When you've finished reading them,
you take them back so others can borrow them,"
says Daddy Pig.

He looks at the book.

"I have had this for a rather long time," Daddy Pig says.

"You can return it tomorrow," says Mummy Pig,

"but right now, it's bedtime."

"After Daddy reads this story!"

Peppa insists.

Daddy Pig begins to read:

"The Wonderful World of Concrete.
Concrete is made of sand, water, and other things.
Chapter One: Sand!"

Sounds of snoring fill the room.
Peppa and George are fast asleep.

So is Mummy Pig!

The next morning,
Peppa and her family head to the library.

Peppa can't believe how many books are on the shelves.
"Look at them all!" she shouts.

"Shhh, Peppa," says Daddy Pig.
"You must be quiet in the library,
because people come here
to read and to be quiet."

"Next, please!"

comes another shout.
It's Miss Rabbit, the librarian.

"Hello, Mummy Pig," she says.
"Are you returning these books?"

"Yes, Miss Rabbit." Mummy Pig gives her
books to Miss Rabbit to scan, and the
computer beeps as the books slide across
the counter.

"Why is the computer beeping?" asks Peppa.

"It's checking to see that you haven't been naughty
and kept the book for too long."

"I may have kept this book for a bit too long,"
says Daddy Pig.

"Don't worry,"
says Miss Rabbit.

Then her computer
makes a loud, long
beep. "Daddy Pig!" she
shouts. "You've had
this book out for ten
years!"

"Naughty
Daddy!"
says Peppa.

Now that Daddy Pig's book is returned, he can borrow another one.
Peppa and George want to borrow books, too.

Miss Rabbit shows Peppa and George
to the children's section.

"Ooh!" says Peppa.
"There are books about
princesses, and animals, and planets!"

110

Danny Dog and Suzy Sheep are at the library, too. Danny Dog is borrowing a book about soccer. Suzy Sheep is borrowing one about doctors.

George has chosen his book. It's about dinosaurs! "Dine-saw!" says George.

"Grrr!"

Daddy Pig has found an exciting new book:
Further Adventures in the *World of Concrete*.

"But Daddy Pig," says Peppa,

"I want a fun bedtime book!"

Mummy Pig pulls out a Red Monkey book.
"Not that again!" says Peppa. "It's boring."

"It's a different story," says Mummy Pig.
"Once upon a time, there was a red monkey—"

"I know," says Peppa.
"He had a bath,
brushed his teeth,
and went to sleep," she says.

"No," says Mummy Pig.
"He had **adventures!**"

"Ooh!" say the children.

They all gather around to see the book.

Peppa wants to hear the story.
"We can read it at home," says Mummy Pig.

"But I already chose a book about a princess," says Peppa.
Then she sees another book, about birds.
"That book looks interesting, too!"

Miss Rabbit has good news for Peppa:
"You can take up to three books home, if you'd like!"

"Yippee!" says Peppa.

"You just have to remember
to bring them back on time,"
says Miss Rabbit.
"And that goes for you, too,
Daddy Pig."

Peppa laughs. "I'll make sure he remembers.
I want to come back to the library all the time.
I love the library!"

Back at home, it's bedtime.

Mummy Pig opens the new Red Monkey book.

"Once upon a time, there was a red monkey.

He jumped in a space rocket and went to the moon."

"The moon!"
says Peppa.
"What an adventure!"

Mummy Pig turns the page.

"He had a picnic with a dinosaur."

"Dine-saw!" says George.

"Then the red monkey swam under the sea."

Mummy Pig turns the last page.

"Finally, he climbed the highest mountain.

That was a busy day!"

"I think Daddy Pig agrees," says Peppa.
Everyone looks. Daddy Pig is fast asleep.

"The end," whispers Mummy Pig. Sounds of Daddy
Pig's snores fill the room. Everyone laughs.

What a fun day!

Peppa Pig

and the

Day at the Museum

At breakfast, Mummy and Daddy Pig have a surprise.
"We have a special day planned," says Mummy Pig.

"We're going to a museum!"

"What is a museum?" asks Peppa.

"It's a place full of interesting things.
Sometimes those things are very old," says Daddy.

"Older than you?" asks Peppa.

"Yes," says Daddy, "even older than me."

"Here we are!" says Mummy Pig.

"The museum is very big," says Peppa.

"Oooh," says George.

Mummy and Daddy Pig buy tickets from Miss Rabbit.

"What would you like to see first?" asks Miss Rabbit.

"Jewels!" cries Peppa.

"Dine-saw," says George. "Grrrr."

127

The first stop is the Kings and Queens room.

It is full of things from long ago.

Peppa likes the beautiful robes.

And look. There's a crown!

There is a throne, too. Peppa wishes she could sit on it.
She imagines what it would be like to be the Queen,
to wear the crown, and sit on the royal throne.

"If I were the Queen," she says, "I would eat cake every day."

The family bows to her royal highness, Queen Peppa.

George does not want to wear a crown and sit on the throne.

He wants to see the dinosaurs.

George stands at the doorway to the
dinosaur room.

There are many unusual creatures here.

"Everything is so big," says Peppa,
in a very big voice.

"Ooh," says George, in a very small voice.

George sees a **big** dinosaur.

"Don't worry," says Daddy.
"Those are just dinosaur *bones*."

They may just be bones, but they are **very big.**

George can just imagine what it would be like to be a dinosaur.
He would be bigger than Peppa.

He could chase her!

George sees something smaller and not very scary.

It's a robot dinosaur!

Everyone is hungry, so they go to the museum café for cake.
After the snack, it's time to see the next exhibit.

"There's a special one at the museum today," says Mummy Pig.
"It's all about space."

George's friend Edmond is at the museum, too.
Edmond knows a lot about space.

He and George wear space helmets to tour the exhibit.
Miss Rabbit gives them their tickets.

First, everyone gets on board the space ride.

"Blast off!" says Mr. Rabbit. He is the tour guide.

"This is just pretend, isn't it?" asks Peppa.

"Yes," says Mr. Rabbit, "it's just pretend."

The rocket takes them to the pretend moon.
There are pretend planets, too.
"Do you know what the planets are made of?"
asks Mr. Rabbit.

"Cardboard!" says Peppa.

"Well, these models are made out of cardboard,
but the real planets are made out of other things."

"Rock and ice and gas," says Edmond.

"What about cheese?" asks Daddy Pig.
"I thought the moon was made out of cheese!"

"That's just silly, Daddy," says Peppa.

"If this was the real moon, you could jump over my head," says Mr. Rabbit. "Do you know why?"

"There's less gravity!" yells Edmond.

"You're right! We can make you feel like
you're on the moon with these special big rubber bands."

Everybody straps into the rubber bands. They jump —
BOING, BOING, BOING — just like on the moon!
Miss Rabbit takes their picture.

At the gift shop,
Peppa gets the picture
of everyone jumping
on the pretend moon.

Daddy is hungry again,
so he gets a piece
of moon cheese!

Then it's time
to go home.
It has been a great
day at the museum.

Later, Mummy Pig asks Peppa and George,
"What was your favorite thing at the museum?"

Peppa liked everything at the museum,
but she does have a favorite.
"The crown!" says Peppa.

George liked the space ride,
but that wasn't his favorite.
"Dine-saw!" says George.

"I have two favorites," says Daddy Pig.
"The cake and the cheese!"

Peppa Pig

and the
Treasure Hunt

Peppa Pig and her little brother, George, are very excited.
They are going to spend the day with Granny Pig and Grandpa Pig.

"Off we go!"
says Daddy Pig.

"Hello, Peppa. Hello, George!" says Granny Pig.
"Ahoy there, me hearties!" says Grandpa.

"We have a surprise for you!"
Granny and Grandpa Pig say.

Peppa and George love surprises.
"It's a treasure hunt!" says Granny Pig.

"Grandpa buried treasure somewhere in the yard.
It's up to you two to find it."

Treasure!

George wants to find it. Peppa wants to find it, too.

Peppa has never searched for treasure before.
"How do we find it?" she asks.

"Follow the map!" says Granny.

"Hooray!"
says Peppa.

Grandpa Pig gives George the pirate hat.

"Arrr,"

says George.

Something isn't quite right.
"I don't understand the map,"
says Peppa. "Can you help,
Daddy?"

"Oh, yes," says Daddy
Pig. "I'm very good
with maps.
Hmmm, this map *is*
difficult."

"You're holding it upside down,"
says Granny Pig.

"Whoops!" says Daddy. Everyone laughs.

"I see," says Peppa. "It's easy.
X marks the spot where the treasure is buried!
It's right between two apple trees.
But where are they?"

"You have to find the clues," says Granny Pig.
"The first one is in a bottle."

Peppa and George search.
They find a scarecrow.

They find butterflies.

They find frogs.

George finds something else.

"That's not treasure," says Peppa.

"I see it!" cries Peppa. She and George rush down into the yard. "It's a message in a bottle!"

Peppa hands the message to Mummy Pig to read. "This pirate has very bad handwriting," says Mummy Pig. "I can't make it out at all."

"Nonsense," says Grandpa Pig.

"It says to find the arrows and follow them."

Peppa and George follow the arrows to the tree house,

past the chicken coop,

and behind the beehive.

They follow them up, down,
and all around the yard.

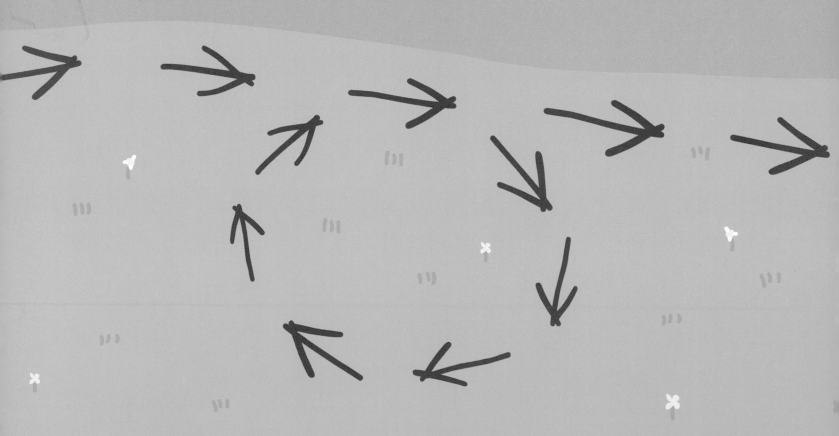

170

At the last arrow, Peppa sees something bright and shiny on the ground. "A key!"

"I wonder what it will unlock," says Peppa.

Peppa looks up. She points.
"An apple tree!" she says.

George points, and Peppa says,
"Another apple tree!"

Daddy gets a shovel.
He digs and digs
and digs.
Finally the shovel hits
something hard.

"What is it?" asks Peppa. Daddy reaches down into the hole. . . .

"A treasure chest!"

cries Peppa.

"Oooh,"

says George.

Peppa uses the key to unlock the chest. It is filled with shiny coins.

"Gold coins," says Peppa. "We're rich!"

"Oooh," says George.

"These are better than gold coins," says Grandpa Pig.
"These coins are made of chocolate."

"OOOOH!" say Peppa and George.

"**Mmmm,**" says Peppa.
"This is the best treasure ever!"